Scrump and Friends
Go for a Swim

Dyslexic Friendly Edition

TIF E. BOOTS

Illustrated by Syranity Barker

The story, all names, characters, and incidents portrayed in this book are fictitious. No identification with actual persons (living or deceased), places, buildings, and products is intended or should be inferred.

DF Version ISBN-13: 978-1-963272-25-3

ShelteringTree.Earth, LLC Publishing
PO Box 973, Eagle Lake, FL 33839

Did you enjoy this book?
We love to hear from our readers.
Please visit the author and illustrator at
ShelteringTreeMedia.com

What is a "Dyslexic Friendly" Book?

Sheltering Tree Media has taken steps to make our books more friendly for those who live with dyslexia. While the following principles will not make every book readable for every reader, it is our best effort to create products that encourage reading and to support all readers.

Throughout the book, we use a font named OpenDyslexic. This is a free font that is designed to help dyslexic readers distinguish each letter from the others. For more information about OpenDyslexic, how it differs from other fonts, and research behind the font, visit their website: www.opendyslexic.com.

In our books created for children, we use a font size which provides the reader with plenty of spacing between the letters (which is called kerning). The bigger, wider font tends to be easier to the reader's eyes.

The space between each word is increased (this is called word spacing). This helps better to distinguish when one word ends and the next begins. The line spacing is greater than most common fonts (this is called *leading*). This all should help with readability.

Whenever possible, the text is Left-Aligned but it is not justified on the right side. Allowing the right side of a paragraph to remain *rough* keeps the word spacing consistent throughout.

Our Dyslexic Friendly books are printed on cream or ivory paper which is also thicker than the average book page. This minimizes the sharp contrast of black-on-white pages as well as bleedthrough of text from the previous page.

Finally, Sheltering Tree Media has made colored overlays available when you purchase a book through our online store. You can find these overlays at ShelteringTreeMedia.com/shop/dyslexic-friendly.

These are some of the principles we use to create a book as readable as possible to those living with dyslexia. Some may find this helpful; some may not. Please provide us with any insights you might have to improve our Dyslexic Friendly principles. We pray this will enable many to heighten their love for reading.

DEDICATION

For the Children.
Trying something new can be scary,
but once you learn it can be fun.

CONTENTS

SCRUMP AND FRIENDS GO FOR A SWIM

It was a very hot and sunny day. Brutus and Charlie sat outside of Scrump's rabbit hole.

"Scrump!" they called. "Come out and play."

"Hi, Brutus. Hi, Charlie," Scrump said as he climbed out of his hole. "What do you want to play today?"

"We could play Red Light Green Light," suggested Brutus.

"It's so hot today," said Charlie, looking at the bright blue sky. "We could go to the pond for a swim."

"That's a good idea!" Brutus barked. "We can play Marco Polo."

"Okay," Scrump agreed. "Last one there is a rotten egg!"

"Wait," said Brutus. "We cannot go swimming by ourselves. It is not safe to swim without an adult watching."

"Oh, you're right," agreed Scrump. "Who can we get to watch us? My Dad is helping my mom expand the burrow today."

"We could ask my mom and dad," said Charlie. "But they told me this morning they were going to start foraging and storing our food for the winter. They may not be able to take a break. It usually takes several months to bury all the nuts they find."

"Maybe we could ask Dash?" Brutus suggested. "He is an adult, and he is a really good swimmer. Plus, he is big enough to help all of us if something bad happens."

"That's a good idea," agreed Charlie.

"Let's go find him," said Scrump. "I hope he is not busy; I really want to play in the water today."

Together they ran away from Scrump's tree, over the grass and through the back yard. They raced to the playground and called for Dash. When no one answered them, they ran up to the steps to the big back porch.

"Dash?" Brutus called, looking around. He did not see Dash, just the fat orange cat sunning herself on the porch railing.

"Excuse us, I'm sorry to interrupt your nap. We are looking for Dash. Have you seen him?" asked Brutus.

The orange cat slowly opened one eye and yawned, stretching one clawed paw out in front of her. "I saw him walking towards the garden a little while ago. He likes to carry the weed basket for the missus when she gardens."

"Thank you so much for your help. We will go look there for him," said Scrump.

The friends ran down the steps and stopped at the slope of the hill looking down at the garden. "The grass is super soft and fluffy here," stated Charlie. "Let's see who can roll down it the fastest."

Brutus and Scrump quickly agreed and laid down beside Charlie.

"1...2...3...Go!" counted Brutus.

Giggling and dizzy, they tumbled into a pile at the bottom of the hill.

"That was a lot of fun!" exclaimed Brutus.

"Yeah," said Scrump. "If we can't find Dash to watch us swim, we can come back and roll down the hill some more."

Still a little dizzy, they walked under the cherry tree and through the garden gate. "Dash?" Scrump called.

"Over here!" They heard Dash call back from the far end of the garden. They passed bushes with bright red tomatoes and dark purple eggplants. They also passed heads of lettuce, cabbage, cauliflower, and broccoli.

"Wow," said Scrump. "All these vegetables are going to make me hungry."

Finally, they reached the far end of the garden and found Dash sitting with a basket in his mouth. He was in front of tall stalks of corn. The missus was kneeling with her back to him while picking long green beans. After snapping a few beans from the plant, she would reach back and Dash would bump her hand with the basket. She dropped the beans into the basket and reached to pick some more.

"Hi, Dash," Brutus greeted him while Charlie and Scrump hid in the shadows of the corn. Brutus explained quickly, "We were wondering if you would be able to watch us down at the pond. It is a hot day, and we would like to go for a swim, but we know it is not safe to swim without an adult to watch us."

"It is always best to have an adult to supervise anytime you're near the water," agreed Dash. "I think we are almost done picking vegetables for dinner. After I help carry them back up to the house, I will be happy to watch you guys. I am glad you asked and didn't just go down to the pond by yourselves. You guys head on down that way, and when I'm done, I will meet you there. Do not go onto the beach or near the water until I get there."

"Yeah! Thank you," exclaimed Scrump and Charlie from their hiding spots in the row of corn.

"Yes," Brutus added his thoughts. "Thank you so much. We will see you by the pond, and don't worry, we will not go near the water until you are with us." Brutus turned back to his friends just as the missus reached back with a last hand full of beans.

Together the three friends walked back through the garden and out of the gate. Then they walked slowly to the fence that circled the pond. They talked excitedly about swimming and playing games and tried to predict who would win in a swimming race, while they waited not-so-patiently for Dash.

After a few moments they heard Dash calling. "Ok, kids, I'm here! Go on in. Be careful."

They ran across the wooden dock and into the water with a big splash.

"1

2

3

Not it!"

Scrump shouted as he surfaced.

"Not it!" giggled Brutus, followed by Charlie.

Charlie was the last of his friends to call *not it*, so he closed his eyes and counted:

"1

2

3

4

5

6

7

8

9

10.

Marco?"

"Polo," said Scrump from somewhere in front of him.

"Polo!" said Brutus from behind him.

Charlie dove straight for Scrump's voice and tried to tag his friend. Scrump moved and Charlie missed. With his eyes still closed Charlie listened for his friends. He could hear the splashing and giggling but he could also hear something else.

The sound was soft and hard to hear over the noise his friends were making, but it almost sounded like someone was crying.

"Time out," he said and opened his eyes. Brutus and Scrump quit splashing and looked at Charlie in confusion. Charlie was treading water and looking around the pond. He pointed to the edge of the water near the wooden dock.

Brutus and Scrump looked in the direction Charlie pointed. There, next to the dock, sat a small form. Now that they were quiet, they heard the soft sobs that Charlie had heard during their game. The three friends started swimming to the beach to see if they could help.

Scrump got out of the pond first and was looking at a small green turtle on the sand. "Hi. I'm Scrump," he said. "These are my friends Brutus and Charlie."

The turtle looked up at the three friends, but he didn't smile. Tears flowed down his face.

"Why are you crying?" Scrump asked the turtle.

"My name is Herbie," said the turtle. "You guys look like you're having so much fun; I would like to play too."

"You can play," said Scrump. "More friends are always welcome."

"I do not know how to swim and I'm afraid of the water," sniffled Herbie.

"We could play something else out of the water," suggested Charlie.

"You guys shouldn't have to stop swimming," said Herbie.

"Do you want to try to learn how to swim?" asked Brutus. "The water isn't scary when you know how to be safe around it."

"You always want to have a buddy with you and if you start feeling tired, you need to take a break," Charlie explained.

"We can play in the shallow part of the pond until you are comfortable with the water," Scrump suggested.

"I can teach you how to swim if you want to learn," Brutus offered again. "You can sit on my back, and I can keep you from sinking."

"You would do that for me?" asked Herbie. "I'd like to try. What do I need to do?"

"Swimming is not hard. All you do is kick your feet and reach forward to grab the water in front of you. Pull the water back with one hand and reach for more water with the other hand. The movements keep you moving and floating," explained Brutus.

Herbie looked doubtfully at his new friend, thinking it couldn't be that easy. Then he looked longingly at the pond. He really did want to play in the water with them. He finally decided and said, "Ok. I will try."

"Climb on my back," said Brutus "I will make sure you stay safe while you practice the movements. You will be swimming by yourself in no time.

Brutus laid down so Herbie could climb up his back while Scrump and Charlie helped their new friend when he needed it. Then the four of them walked over the sand and into the pond. When the water touched Herbie's belly, he tried not to be scared. His new friends believed he could do this; he did not want to let them down.

"Start kicking your feet, Herbie," Scrump shouted.

"Reach for the water and pull it towards you," Charlie cheered.

Herbie did as they said, and they continued calling out encouragement. Soon Brutus did not feel Herbie on his back any longer. He looked over his shoulder and could see Herbie slowly swimming behind him.

Herbie kept kicking his feet and pulling water to him. He did not notice that Brutus was no longer under him and that no one was beside him. He forgot to be afraid and just kept swimming. Brutus, Scrump, and Charlie swam up beside him.

"You've got it now. You're swimming by yourself!" exclaimed Brutus.

"Good job!" said Charlie

"Keep it up!" encouraged Scrump.

Herbie looked over; Brutus was next to him and not holding him up! Scrump and Charlie swam on the other side of Herbie. He was swimming all by himself!

Herbie smiled and said, "Not it," as he swam away from his new friends.

"Not it," said Charlie and Scrump.

Brutus was the last to say, "Not it!" He closed his eyes and started to count.

The four friends swam and played on the sand near the water the rest of the day. They found a ball that someone had lost and played with it in the water. They were able to play a swimming version of *Red Light, Green Light*. Even Dash decided to get in the water and play with them for a while.

When the sun started to set, and the air turned cooler they got out of the water.

"Thank you all so much for teaching me how to swim." Herbie said. "I am glad I tried something new. It may have seemed scary but it was a lot of fun."

"Yes," said Dash, "Trying something new can be very scary whether it's an activity like swimming, playing a new game, meeting someone new, or even trying a new food. But you never know what you might miss out on unless you try."

"I want thank you, Dash, for taking the time to supervise us so we could be safe while having fun together today." Brutus said.

"Yes," added Scrump. "Thank you."

"Thanks Dash," said Charlie, "we wouldn't have been as safe while playing today without you."

"Thank you, Dash," said Herbie, I wouldn't have met my new friends without you, or learned to swim."

As the sky continued to darken, the five friends said goodnight and headed back to their homes. They each wondered what surprises and new friends they would find tomorrow.

ABOUT THE AUTHOR

Tif E. Boots wrote her first children's book as a birthday present for her daughter. Many years later it has been shared with her sister, cousins, classmates, and now you.

Tif was raised in Marana, Arizona and was working concession stands at county fairs in Arizona and Michigan with her family until she graduated from Marana High School in 2000. She became a mother and correctional officer in 2004. She then moved to Nevada, Missouri with her family where she was blessed with her second daughter and fell into a career of nurse's assistant for Hospice.

Tif and her family relocated to Mulberry, Florida in 2017. In her free time, Tif can usually be found on the water or at amusement parks spending time with family and friends, and simply enjoying the life that God has blessed her with.

ABOUT THE ILLUSTRATOR

Syranity Barker is an illustrator who has always had a love for art. She was born in Tucson, Arizona and eventually moved to central Florida where she graduated high school.

Syranity illustrated her love of drawing early in life; her family were great supporters of her passions and always made sure she had a variety of supplies and mediums. While she was still in high school, her work was entered in numerous art shows. She received the *City Commissioners Choice Award* for a mixed media portrait of her dog and has sold several pieces of her work.

Still fresh out of high school, Syranity works two jobs and illustrates professionally in her spare time. She is currently the in-house illustrator for *Sheltering Tree.Earth Publishing* and also promotes herself as a free-lance artist.

Syranity enjoys singing, skating, spending time with her friends and family, and creating her own characters and writing backstories for them.

Syranity aspires to become an art teacher and share her passion for drawing and self-expression with others.

DISCUSSION GUIDE FOR
SMALL GROUPS, CLASSES, AND
INDIVIDUAL REFLECTION

DIRECTIONS: Write your answers on the lines. In the space below the lines, draw a picture explaining your answer.

1. Who calls to Scrump from outside his hole? Why?

_____

_____

_____

_____

2. Why do they decide to go swimming?

3. Who is the last one to say *not it?*

_____

_____

_____

4. What game are they playing and who does Charlie try to catch first?

_____

_____

_____

_____

_____

_____

_____

_____

5. What does Charlie hear?

6. Why does he call for a timeout?

7. Who is crying and why?

8. How do the friends help Herbie?

9. Do you think they explained how to swim well enough for someone to understand?

10. How did they help Herbie with his fears?

11. Do you think that swimming can be scary? Why or why not?

12. What else do you think would be scary to learn to do?

13. What is your favorite thing to play in the water?

14. What other games do they play through the day?

_____

_____

_____

_____

_____

_____

_____

_____

15. What do you think the friends will do the next day?

SWIMMING SAFETY RESOURCES

10 Golden Rules of Water Safety and Drowning
Prevention. SwimJim, LLC, 2019.
https://swimjim.com/10-golden-rules-water-
safety-drowning-prevention/

Anne Wahlgren, 10 Water safety rules to teach
your children. June 3, 2019.
https://printableparents.com/10-water-
safety-rules-to-teach-your-children/

Healthy Swimming Fact Sheets. CDC Center for
Disesase Control and Prevention.
https://www.cdc.gov/healthywater/swimmin
g/materials/fact-sheets.html

How to Swim Safely in Rivers and Other Natural
Environments https://www.redcross.org/get-
help/how-to-prepare-for-emergencies/types-
of-emergencies/water-safety/lake-river-
safety.html

Open Water Safety https://ndpa.org/10-open-water-safety-tips/

Scott Stueber. 15 *Pool Safety Tips to keep you and your family safe.* Jun 25, 2013 WestBend Cares Blog. https://www.thesilverlining.com/westbendcares/blog/bid/182094/

SHELTERING TREE

Earth Publishing

SheIteringTreeMedia.com

For more information,
to become one of our authors,
translators, or illustrators,
or to contact the author or illustrator:

SheIteringTreeMedia.com

www.ingramcontent.com/pod-product-compliance
Lightning Source LLC
Chambersburg PA
CBHW060754180626
46818CB00002B/569